QUIRKY TIMES AT QUAGMIRE CASTLE

BY KAREN WALLACE

ILLUSTRATED BY HELEN FLOOK

Librarian Reviewer
Kathleen Baxter
Children's Literature Consultant
formerly with Anoka County Library, MN
BA College of Saint Catherine, St. Paul, MN
MA in Library Science, University of Minnesota

Reading Consultant
Elizabeth Stedem
Educator/Consultant, Colorado Springs, CO
MA in Elementary Education, University of Denver, CO

STONE ARCH BOOKS
Minneapolis   San Diego

First published in the United States in 2007
by Stone Arch Books,
151 Good Counsel Drive, P.O. Box 669,
Mankato, Minnesota 56002.
www.stonearchbooks.com

Originally published in Great Britain in 2003
by A & C Black Publishers Ltd,
38 Soho Square, London, W1D 3HB.

Library of Congress Cataloging-in-Publication Data
Wallace, Karen.
    Quirky Times at Quagmire Castle / by Karen Wallace; illustrated by
Helen Flook.
    p. cm. — (Pathway Books)
    Summary: When Jack and Emily learn that Quagmire Castle, their
beloved, crumbling home, is going to be sold, they seek help from their
ghostly ancestors, who are only too delighted to be of service.
    ISBN-13: 978-1-59889-112-6 (hardcover)
    ISBN-10: 1-59889-112-X (hardcover)
    ISBN-13: 978-1-59889-263-5 (paperback)
    ISBN-10: 1-59889-263-0 (paperback)
    [1. Castles—Fiction. 2. Ghosts—Fiction. 3. Magic—Fiction.] I. Flook,
Helen, ill. II. Title.
PZ7.W1568Qui 2007
[Fic]—dc22   2006005083

Art Director: Heather Kindseth
Graphic Designer: Kay Fraser

1 2 3 4 5 6 11 10 09 08 07 06

TABLE OF CONTENTS

CHAPTER 1

"Something's on Aunt Tabitha's mind," said Jack Nightshade as he and his sister, Emily, sat in a rowboat on Toad Lake.

It was a warm, summer day at Quagmire Castle, and the sound of a sewing machine hummed through the air.

"She's been sewing for two days now," added Jack.

Emily looked down at a water lily. A huge green frog with golden eyes was watching her.

No matter how hard she stared at it, the frog showed no sign of being frightened. It was almost as if it was listening to what they was saying.

"Do you think we should ask?" said Emily. "Last time this happened, it turned out she was sewing a cover for the roof." She grinned. "Maybe she's found a way to sew new windows for the tower."

Jack dipped the oars in the soupy green water and shook his head. "I think it's more than that. Yesterday, I went down to the kitchen and Mrs. Gristle the cook told me that Aunt Tabitha is only eating sardine sandwiches."

"Ugh!" Emily made a face. "What on earth for?"

"She said it was good for her brain and she needed all the help she could get." Jack shook his head. "There's something wrong, I'm sure there is."

There was a loud *plop*! Emily looked down. The big frog had disappeared.

* * *

In the West Tower of the castle, Delicia Nightshade stared at her silvery fingers. She tried to remember the days when she could see her reflection in the mirror.

It was a long time ago, far too many years to count.

Anyway, judging from her beautiful hands and ankles, Delicia was sure she was still as beautiful as she had been in those long ago days.

Those ancient days, when she traveled by coach and her servants were dressed in velvet and silk in the Nightshade colors of black and red.

Delicia sighed. It wasn't that she wanted to go back in time.

She liked living in the West Tower of Quagmire Castle. Nobody bothered them.

Besides, she had Dudley for company

Delicia sighed and floated over to the window. Dudley hadn't returned from one of his little adventures.

Dudley had taught himself to change into anything he wanted. These days he was always turning into a frog.

And since it had been his idea years ago to dig a lake for the castle, he had decided to take a closer look at how the water lilies were doing.

At that moment, Dudley suddenly appeared by her side.

Water dripped from his hair and a weed hung from his ear.

Delicia made a face. This was the second time he had gone off somewhere in his best clothes. "They'll shrink, you know," she said, trying not to sound too angry at her husband.

"No, they won't," cried Dudley, peering out the window. "They'll grow. They're only little because we see them from way up here."

Delicia stared at her husband as if he were crazy. "Have you been drinking that green stuff again?" she asked.

"Certainly not," replied Dudley.

He pointed down at Jack and Emily, who were crossing the lawn.

"I was talking about the little ones who live in the house," he said.

He pulled the weed off his ear. "You see, I was sitting on a water lily, just quietly listening—"

At that moment, a monkey with shiny gray fur jumped through the air. It spun three times, and landed upside-down on the floor.

Dudley and Delicia stared at the monkey, and then at each other. They were both thinking the same thing.

When Powderball spun three times and landed upside-down it was a sure sign that something was wrong.

And it had something to do with Quagmire Castle.

CHAPTER 2

Jack and Emily stood in the middle of Aunt Tabitha's sitting room and stared at the plates of sardine sandwiches stacked up on the tables.

It was clear to both of them that if Aunt Tabitha had been hoping to improve her brainpower, it wasn't working.

Aunt Tabitha looked up from her desk. "Sit down, dears," she said in a tired voice. "I'm afraid I have some bad news to tell you."

Jack and Emily looked at each other and quickly sat down on the sofa.

"Gordon Grabbit, the bank manager, came to see me," said Aunt Tabitha.

"He won't give me any more money to look after Quagmire Castle. He wants me to sell."

"Oh, no!" cried Jack.

Emily turned white as a sheet.

"I've tried and tried to think of a way to solve the problem," said Aunt Tabitha. "But I haven't come up with any answers so far. And we are very quickly running out of time."

She picked up a huge pile of papers. "You see, after paying the bank the money I owe them for giving me loans in the first place, I haven't got any money left to pay the bills."

"I don't understand," said Jack. "Why is Mr. Grabbit being so mean?"

"Bank managers don't think like we do," said Aunt Tabitha with a sigh. "I'm sure that when he looks at Quagmire Castle, all he sees is a ruin that should be pulled down."

"What are you going to do, Aunt Tabitha?" asked Jack.

"I'm going to sew a cover for Toad Lake," replied Aunt Tabitha firmly. "The old one is full of holes and, as you know, sometimes I have my best ideas when I am sewing."

Emily looked up. "Can we help?"

"We'll do anything!" said Jack.

Aunt Tabitha forced herself to smile. "Perhaps if all three of us think as hard as we can, one of us will come up with a good idea."

Then she shook her head as if she had suddenly remembered something. "There is one other problem," she said.

Jack and Emily stared at her. "What?"

"We don't have much time," said Aunt Tabitha. "Gordon Grabbit's coming back next week."

* * *

Jack and Emily slowly climbed the stairs to the second floor.

"How about a yard sale?" said Emily. "We could raise money that way."

"Not enough," muttered Jack. "Someone would have to give us a giant sack of gold."

"How about a raffle?" asked Emily.

"What could we raffle?" asked Jack. "We'd need an emerald the size of a chicken egg."

"Then you come up with some ideas!" cried Emily.

They had reached the top of the stairs on the third floor.

Suddenly, Jack froze and pointed. "What's that?" he said.

A strange monkey was sitting on the hall carpet.

It had shiny gray fur and orange eyes. As soon as it saw Jack and Emily, it jumped into the air, bounced off the walls, and landed on its hands.

Then it stared at them and did handsprings down the hallway.

"Jack," whispered Emily, "I think this monkey wants us to follow him."

Jack looked puzzled. "There's nowhere to go. The hallway is a dead end."

"Let's follow him anyway," whispered Emily quietly.

At that moment, a door they had never seen before appeared in the wall in front of them.

The door was heavy and had a big iron lock. Jack was just about to put his hand out to see if it was real when the monkey walked through it.

To their surprise, Emily and Jack walked through the door, too!

They found themselves at the bottom of a stone staircase.

The monkey ran up the steps and they followed after him.

When they were both almost dizzy from climbing, another door appeared in front of them.

The monkey tapped out a signal: two short knocks, then a pause, followed by two more knocks.

A second later the door swung open.

Even though they knew it was rude to stare, Jack and Emily stared until they thought their eyes would pop out. In front of them stood a man and a woman.

The woman was dressed in a black gown. Her white hair hung down to her shoulders like the mane of a pony.

Beside her was a man with long, curly hair, wearing a black and red jacket with puffy sleeves. A sword hung from his belt. His eyes glowed like coals in his wide face.

Jack closed his eyes and thought.

He had seen these two people before, but where? He couldn't think.

Suddenly, he remembered.

"Are you the people in the paintings downstairs?" he asked.

"Greetings, human children, and welcome!" cried the man with the sword. "Lord Dudley Nightshade at your service! And this is my wife, Lady Delicia."

"Right on! Way to go!" Delicia Nightshade waved Jack and Emily inside.

Delicia read the magazines that people sometimes tossed over the garden walls. She wanted to use modern words to make these young people feel comfortable.

Emily looked around. The strange monkey was nowhere to be seen.

"Don't worry about Powderball," said Delicia.

She put her silvery hand on Emily's shoulder. "Now, let's talk. We really don't have a lot of time," she said.

Emily stared at Delicia's blue eyes. "Can you read minds?" the girl asked.

"Of course! We can do just about anything," Delicia said.

Dudley led the way to a group of chairs. He pushed a table covered in cards to one side. The four sat down.

"We started that game in 1597," said Delicia happily.

"Excuse me," said Emily. "But are you saying you've lived here since 1597?"

"Quagmire Castle is our home," said Delicia.

Her silvery face became serious. "And we want it to stay that way," she said. "That's why we sent Powderball to find you two."

Jack stared at them. "How do you know about Gordon Grabbit?" he asked.

"I turned myself into a frog and listened to you talking on the lake," said Dudley. "Then I turned into a spider and crouched under your aunt's desk."

"And I was a fly," said Delicia.

Emily looked between Jack and Dudley. She noticed that they both had the same wide face and bright eyes.

It was the strangest feeling in the world to find out that your brother looked just like a ghost.

Jack leaned forward on his chair. "Then you know that Aunt Tabitha has to come up with some money by next week or that horrible man will force her to sell."

"I've taken care of that," replied Delicia. "There's a sack of gold at the end of a rope tied to your rowboat. She can pay him off with that for the time being."

She paused. "Would you care for some mead?" she asked. "It's an old recipe of my grandmother's. She got it at a staging post on her way once to Scotland."

"What's mead?" asked Emily.

"What's a staging post?" asked Jack.

Delicia and Dudley looked at each other. Don't children learn anything in schools these days? they wondered.

"Mead is a drink made from honey," said Delicia.

"And a staging post is where someone stops to rest and change horses," explained Dudley.

"You mean like a hotel?" asked Jack.

"Exactly!" cried Delicia. "Just like a country house hotel."

There was a dull thud as Powderball fell off his stool.

It was a sure sign that something important had happened. The room fell completely silent.

Jack and Emily and Delicia and Dudley looked at each other. They all knew they were thinking the same thing.

Quagmire Castle . . . **country house hotel**! It was a stroke of genius!

As far as Delicia and Dudley were concerned, a hotel was a lot more fun than playing cards in the attic.

Even though Jack and Emily didn't know it yet, Delicia and Dudley had made a decision.

Their time had come at last!

CHAPTER 3

Delicia tried to stop her feet from tapping on the floor.

Making plans was one of her favorite things to do, and over the past five hundred years she had gotten quite a lot of practice.

"We can do almost anything," she said happily, looking at Jack and Emily.

"To save Quagmire Castle," added Dudley. "That's the most important thing of all."

Jack looked at the two strange people in front of him. "I hope you don't mind me saying this," he said, "but nowadays things have changed."

He paused. "You see, most people are frightened of ghosts. I mean, you are ghosts, aren't you?"

"Phantoms! Spirits! Ghosts! Call us what you like," cried Delicia happily. "Yes indeed, we are completely different from the normal, human world."

"But as I said, we can change into anything," explained Dudley.

Delicia smiled proudly at her husband. "And not just animals. We can do humans, too," she said.

She turned to Jack and Emily and winked. "So you see, we could be really useful and if something gets tricky, all we do is—"

Delicia and Dudley disappeared. Jack and Emily looked at each other.

It was so weird that neither of them could think of anything to say.

"First things first," said Jack. "Let's see if there really is a sack of gold hidden in Toad Lake!"

* * *

"Goodness me!" Aunt Tabitha said. "This is too wonderful! I do believe I shall have to sit down!"

On the floor in the middle of her room was a wet sack full of gold coins.

As Jack had said, and it was only a little lie, it must have been there for hundreds of years.

It was lucky that their fishing hook had caught the old sack.

"We counted it all, Aunt Tabitha," said Emily. "There's more than enough to stop Mr. Grabbit from forcing you to sell."

"I am curious about your idea of turning Quagmire Castle into a hotel," said Aunt Tabitha. "I do know something about them myself, you know."

"Have you ever stayed in one?" asked Jack, looking at her.

"Certainly not," replied Aunt Tabitha. "They're too expensive! I read all about them the last time I went to the dentist. All you need is a lovely home with a beautiful garden and delicious food."

She smiled. "Then your guests pay you lots and lots of money. What clever children you are!"

"It was Delicia's idea," said Emily.

Jack kicked her under the table and she turned bright red.

"What was that?" Aunt Tabitha asked.

"Delicious food is a really great idea," said Jack.

"Thank you, dear," Aunt Tabitha said.

At that moment, there was a knock on the door.

Mrs. Gristle came into the room. "Mr. Grabbit to see you," Mrs. Gristle said, scowling. "Shall I tell him you're busy?"

"Goodness, no!" cried Aunt Tabitha, standing up. "Show him in. I have something very important to tell him."

* * *

Fifteen minutes later, Gordon Grabbit stood in the room.

He was slapping the leg of his pants with a handful of papers.

He had a face like thunder.

"You'll regret this," he snarled, looking at the lumpy wet sack on the carpet. "Your pile of coins is not going to last long enough to save Quagmire Castle."

"Old gold is just as good as new gold, Mr. Grabbit," said Aunt Tabitha.

"You'll never be able to keep up with your payments," he said.

Gordon Grabbit banged his papers down on the table. "I'll be back again next week."

"That won't be at all necessary," said Aunt Tabitha.

"It certainly will," snapped Grabbit.

"Oh, no it won't," replied Aunt Tabitha. She picked up the papers and threw them into the fire.

"You see, Mr. Grabbit. By the end of next week, I shall never need your bank's money again."

"Ha!" said Gordon Grabbit rudely. "When pigs fly."

At that moment, Jack and Emily saw a large pink pig fly past the window.

Even though it had a curly tail and a snout, there was no way to hide the eyes of Dudley Nightshade!

* * *

That evening, Aunt Tabitha asked everyone to a special business supper in the dining room.

After they had finished eating, she pulled on a rope.

A huge purple banner dropped down from the ceiling.

Quagmire Castle — Open for Business was sewn in huge gold letters across the front.

"You see?" said Aunt Tabitha. "I've been busy."

Jack and Emily stood up with clipboards in their hands. They had also been busy.

If Quagmire Castle was to become a hotel, there was a lot of work to do.

All the bedrooms had to be cleaned and redecorated.

The kitchen had to be made bigger so that Mrs. Gristle could handle preparing the extra food.

And of course, the lawns would have to be mown every day.

As Emily and then Jack read out their lists, everyone's faces grew more and more serious. How on earth would they do it all in time?

Suddenly, there was a knock on the door. Two very strange people walked into the room.

The man was dressed in an old-fashioned suit and carried a ladder and a large bucket.

The woman was wearing a leopard skin leotard with a red cape. In one hand she held a huge feather duster and in the other hand was a set of paints.

Jack and Emily looked at each other and grinned.

Lord Dudley and Lady Delicia Nightshade had finally come downstairs from the attic!

"Good evening, dear lady!" cried Dudley happily.

"I am sorry for the lateness of the hour but we understand you are in need of some help," he said.

Beside him, Delicia's eyes sparkled like rare jewels.

It must have been something in their eyes, thought Emily, later.

It didn't seem strange to Aunt Tabitha or anyone else that two complete strangers turned up in the night and offered to help turn Quagmire Castle into a hotel.

Aunt Tabitha stood up. "Yes we are."

"Dudley," said Dudley, bowing.

"Delicia," said Delicia with a smile.

Aunt Tabitha smiled in return.

Even the serious looks on Mrs. Gristle and Herbert Flubber's faces disappeared.

"Yes, we do need some help. How very kind," said Aunt Tabitha.

She introduced everyone around the table. "This is my nephew, Jack, and niece, Emily. Mrs. Gristle, the cook, and Herbert Flubber, the gardener."

"Charmed," said Delicia.

"Delighted," said Dudley.

They sat down beside Jack and Emily and gave them such big winks and grins that Emily was sure Aunt Tabitha would become suspicious.

But Aunt Tabitha didn't notice a thing.

"How lovely," said Aunt Tabitha, sitting down. "Now, tell me, what can you do to help?"

"We can do everything," said Dudley. "I can run your restaurant." He pointed to his ladder. "I can repaint your castle."

"And I can clean and decorate every room," said Delicia.

"That sounds wonderful," cried Aunt Tabitha. "How long would it take?"

Delicia and Dudley looked puzzled, as if they were trying hard to give the exact right answer.

"Six minutes," said Delicia.

"Six minutes!" cried Aunt Tabitha.

"Six hours," said Dudley.

"Six hours?" asked Mrs. Gristle.

"Six days," said Jack quickly. He stared into Delicia's eyes. "That's what you mean, isn't it?"

"Of course it is!" said Delicia. "Silly me! Six days!" She threw back her head and laughed. "And you'll never even know we're here!"

CHAPTER 4

Several days later, Emily stared at the two paintings of Lord Dudley and Lady Delicia Nightshade that hung in the front hall. "Those two—"

"Ghosts," suggested Jack.

"I know they are ghosts in some ways," said Emily. "In most ways, I guess."

She shook her head. "The thing is, I'm pretty sure they have some crazy ideas and it would be completely impossible to stop them."

At that moment, three paint rollers and a large tray of yellow paint sailed past their heads and flew up the stairs.

They were followed by two vacuum cleaners, three dustpans and brushes, and a long line of feather dusters.

The moment they disappeared, Aunt Tabitha opened her bedroom door.

"You'll never believe what happened," she cried.

Her face was pink with excitement. "I put an ad in the papers two days ago and now we're fully booked!"

She looked around at the newly painted hall and the huge carpet that had appeared overnight. "So I've made a big decision," she said.

A funny feeling tickled the back of Emily's neck.

When Aunt Tabitha made a big decision, something weird always happened.

"We're making such good progress, I've decided to open on Saturday!" she said.

"What?" cried Jack and Emily together. "But—"

"No buts," replied Aunt Tabitha in a happy voice. "I've spoken to Dudley and Delicia and they think it's a great idea."

"What about the kitchen?" asked Emily. "It's still too small."

"Dudley made it bigger last night," said Aunt Tabitha. "At first Mrs. Gristle wasn't sure about cooking over an open fire and she'd never used a spit before. But she soon got the hang of it."

Aunt Tabitha laughed. "She says it's almost faster than a microwave."

"A spit?" said Jack.

"An open fire?" asked Emily.

Aunt Tabitha clapped her hands. "Isn't it so wonderful? Just like a real castle!"

Emily put her hands over her face. "What about fire extinguishers?"

"Dudley thought of that," said Aunt Tabitha. "There's a big bucket of water by the door." She turned. "By the way, have you seen the dining room? Delicia finished it last night."

A moment later, Jack and Emily stood in the dining room and stared.

On one wall were heads of wild animals with tusks and antlers. Spears and armor decorated another wall.

And on another wall, huge carrots were splattered with hundreds of smashed green peas.

"Delicia's so clever," said Aunt Tabitha. "Even vegetarians will love eating here."

Before Jack and Emily could reply, the telephone rang and Aunt Tabitha hurried out of the room.

"I think we'd better look upstairs," said Jack. He was worried.

Emily nodded. "Do you think they put everyone under a spell?"

"Everyone but us," replied Jack.

* * *

Dudley knew all about mazes.

After all, he had made the first one at Quagmire Castle.

Now, the new maze walls were so high that you could get lost if you took the wrong turn. Dudley chuckled to himself. Every turn was the wrong turn.

What Dudley didn't know much about was making flowerbeds. He had always left that sort of thing up to Delicia. Now here he was on his own, trying to remember the best shape for a garden.

In the end, he had decided on his favorite shape. It was the easiest thing to do and now he thought it looked great.

Dudley turned himself into a vulture and sat on the roof to admire his work.

Four flowerbeds in the shape of a skull and crossbones were planted in his favorite colors. Red and black stripes with white for the skull part, of course.

Dudley flapped over the lawn that Herbert Flubber was mowing. Poor Herbert! He took one look at the vulture circling above him and drove his lawnmower straight into Toad Lake!

* * *

"Don't be silly," snapped Gordon Grabbit. "That couldn't be a vulture. I say it's a pigeon."

"If I say it's a vulture, it's a vulture," said his older sister, Cynthia, sitting in the passenger seat. She turned to her husband, who sat in the back, carving his initials into the car's leather seat.

"Isn't that right, Eddy?" said Cynthia.

"Of course it is," said Eddy. "But we're not here to go bird-watching."

Gordon Grabbit turned bright red. All his life he had wanted to impress his older sister. Ever since she got into the housing business and became a millionaire overnight, Gordon wanted to become a millionaire, too.

Quagmire Castle was supposed to be his big chance. "It's perfect," he had told his sister. "Crumbling old castle, lots of land. Fill in the lake and bingo! Fifty houses with their own backyards!"

Cynthia Swipe squinted her piggy eyes. "What about the owner?"

"The old lady owes the bank a lot of money," Gordon Grabbit said. "All I have to do is ask for the full payment. We'll make tons of money!"

Now he stared at the purple banner with the huge gold letters.

Quagmire Castle

Open for Business

Anger flowed through his body. He'd been cheating Tabitha Nightshade out of money for as long as he could remember. How dare she ruin his plans now!

Eddy Swipe picked at a gold tooth with the point of his knife. "So what are we going to do?" he asked.

"I'll think of something," said Cynthia.

"Like what?" he asked.

Cynthia gave her husband an evil smile. "Like, I booked us into the best room on the first night."

She shrugged. "Who knows, maybe the place will get flooded because someone leaves the bathtub running."

Eddy Swipe's three gold teeth sparkled in the sun.

Cynthia's fat face gleamed. "There's only one way to make money and that's the dirty way." She turned to her brother. "Got it, Gordon?"

"Got it, sis," said Gordon Grabbit.

Above them the vulture listened carefully. His black eyes flashed with anger. No one noticed as he flew back toward the castle.

CHAPTER 5

Emily was carrying a huge bunch of red and white roses she had picked from the flowerbeds when she saw Powderball bouncing at the end of the hallway.

"Oh, no," she said out loud.

"What's the matter?" asked Jack. He had just hung another huge banner from the roof.

Emily pointed at Powderball. He was bouncing up and down.

"He wants us to follow him, but the first guests are supposed to arrive in half an hour," said Emily.

Jack stared into the monkey's bright orange eyes. "Come on," said Jack. "If there's trouble, we better find out now."

Emily dropped the bunch of roses into a bucket of water that had mysteriously appeared at her feet. She ran after Jack as fast as she could.

Five minutes later, she sat on a stool, watching as Dudley walked back and forth, waving his sword angrily.

"This Gordon Grabbit," he shouted. "Who did you say he was?"

"Aunt Tabitha's bank manager," replied Jack.

Even though he had always thought Gordon Grabbit was mean, Jack never thought he was a real cheat.

If what Dudley had heard while he was turned into a vulture was true, then Aunt Tabitha must be warned.

"She won't believe you," said Delicia, reading his mind. "It will only upset her on the opening night. Especially since Mrs. Gristle is making a banquet to welcome the new guests. We'll have to take care of this ourselves."

"What will we do?" asked Emily.

"I don't know yet," replied Delicia with a faraway look in her eye. "But I know one thing. No one is knocking down Quagmire Castle."

There was a bang. Through the window, they could see some red smoke coming from the woods. "That's Herbert Flubber's signal," cried Jack. "The guests have just come through the gates. We've got to go!"

"Keep your eyes peeled," warned Dudley. "And don't worry, we'll be around if anything goes wrong."

Two minutes later, Aunt Tabitha stood in the front hall.

"Mrs. Gristle has just left. She got sick!" cried Aunt Tabitha.

Emily's hands flew to her face. "What will we do about the dinner?"

As she spoke, Delicia strolled out of the dining room, dressed in a black and purple dress.

Beside her, Dudley wore a chef's hat. A long silver knife glittered in his hand.

"Tea?" asked Delicia, holding out a tray of tea, milkshakes, and a plate of little cakes.

"Don't worry about a thing," said Dudley. "I'm a genius in the kitchen!"

At that moment, the front door opened and Simon and Sybil Breadsop stood in the doorway with their children, Norman and Trixie.

"See?" said Norman to his sister. "What did I say?" He looked at the hall. "Dumb and boring." He blew a bubble of gum that burst with a big, wet pop.

Jack and Emily stared at each other. They had never seen such horrible children in their lives. Even Aunt Tabitha seemed upset.

"Welcome to Quagmire Castle!" cried Delicia. "May I offer you some refreshment?"

Norman and Trixie made a grab for milkshakes. But as soon as their fingers touched the glass, they jumped back as if they were electrified.

"Perhaps your parents might like theirs first," said Delicia.

Mr. and Mrs. Breadsop picked up the tea cups with shaking hands.

"Why not visit our maze?" suggested Delicia. "A little peace and quiet after your long drive will do you a whole world of good."

Sybil and Simon Breadsop gave Delicia a look of thanks and walked out of the house and into the garden.

"What about us?" Norman gulped his milkshake and slammed the glass down on the tray. "It's our vacation, too."

"Yeah," said Trixie. "And you don't even have a swimming pool."

"We have a big lake," said Emily.

"Who wants to look at a smelly old lake?" Trixie kicked at the carpet.

"Would a playground be better?" asked Delicia.

"Maybe," said Trixie.

"Wonderful!" said Delicia. "Jack will take your suitcases to your rooms." She smiled like a cat. "And I will show you the playground."

"It better be good," said Norman.

"It's out of this world," replied Delicia.

Emily was about to ask what playground Delicia was talking about, but the front door opened again. Cynthia Swipe clicked into the hall on her high-heeled shoes.

Eddy slipped in behind her.

As soon as Emily saw Cynthia's piggy eyes, she knew that these were the people Dudley had warned them about.

"Nice place you got here," said Eddy.

Cynthia held out her hand. "Hi. My name is Cynthia Swipe. And this is Eddy, my husband."

Aunt Tabitha shook their hands. There was something strange about these people but she wasn't sure what it was. It was almost as if she had met them before.

"Do you mind if we tour your place?" asked Eddy. "There's a maze, I believe, and a lake?"

Delicia stepped forward. "Allow me to guide you." She turned to Trixie and Norman. "I was about to show our younger guests the castle's outdoor activity center."

"She means playground," said Trixie in a sour voice.

"Is that what I mean?" asked Delicia. "Will you join us, Mrs. Swipe?" With a wave of her hand, she led them all out the front hall.

Jack and Emily and Aunt Tabitha stood for a moment in silence.

"Our first guests!" said Aunt Tabitha in a nervous voice.

"By the way, I forgot to ask you. Where did you meet Dudley and Delicia?"

"Oh, they were just hanging around," said Emily.

"Ah," said Aunt Tabitha as if that explained everything. "Well, lucky for us." Then she walked through the door to the kitchen.

Car tires crunched on the driveway.

Emily ran to the front door and pulled it open. "Welcome to Quagmire Castle," she said in her friendliest voice.

Two new visitors, Damian Sponge and Velveteen Gray, had arrived.

Damian took his bag out of the trunk of his dark green sports car.

Beside him, Velveteen flipped her coat over her arm. She carefully lifted up her own suitcase.

Neither of them noticed the white card that fluttered to the ground.

"Coffee will be served in the garden room. The dinner will be held in the dining room," said Jack when they had signed in.

Velveteen wrinkled her nose. "Do you have a vegetarian menu?" she asked.

"Yes, dear lady," cried Dudley who had appeared out of nowhere and was now dressed like a waiter. "We even have vegetables on the walls, so you will feel right at home. Let me show you to your rooms," he said.

"Thank you," said Velveteen with a giggle. She stared into Dudley's dark eyes.

It was amazing! She skipped up the stairs as if she had springs in her feet.

Behind her, Damian couldn't believe his eyes. He had never seen Velveteen so happy. He didn't know it was possible.

Emily stood on the front steps. As she stared at the walls of the maze and the green lawn, her eye caught sight of a small white card lying by the wheel of Damian Sponge's car.

She ran over and picked it up. What she read made her heart pound like a hammer. "Sponge and Gray, Hotel Inspectors." Emily stuffed the card in her pocket and ran to find Jack.

It was important that everything went smoothly on their first night. A bad report from the inspectors would mean disaster for Quagmire Castle!

CHAPTER 6

Cynthia and Eddy Swipe watched happily as Norman chopped at the playground equipment with an axe he had found in a garden shed.

Earlier, Trixie had impressed them by snapping through the chains on the swings with a bolt cutter.

Whoever used the swings next would fall and hurt themselves.

"These youngsters could be very useful," said Cynthia. "They've got the right attitude. I noticed it right away when we met them."

"What do you mean?" asked Eddy.

"We'll get them to do the dirty work for us," said Cynthia. She smiled. "They can wreck the place while we're at the stupid dinner tonight."

A large dragonfly zoomed past her face and landed on the grass at her feet. "Like I said, all it takes is a few water faucets turned on and a little more fun with the axe and the bolt cutter," she said.

Eddy grinned and his gold teeth sparkled in the sun. "You're a genius."

"I know," said Cynthia. She got up and headed toward the noise of splintering wood. "Let's go and introduce ourselves," she said. Then she smiled.

Five minutes later, the deal was made.
"Just remember," said Eddy as he handed
Norman and Trixie each a stack of
money. "The job has to be done tonight."

Norman grinned. "We didn't have anything else planned, did we, sis?"

"Sounds like our kind of fun." Trixie looked up from folding her money. "Can we burn the place, too? We like fires."

"Don't be dumb," said her brother. "We're going to flood it, remember?"

"Oh yeah," Trixie said.

"And break a few things," added Norman. Trixie nodded happily.

"After the dinner, let's meet upstairs in our room," said Eddy. He laughed. "Or what's left of it."

Norman and Trixie nodded and walked off into the garden. Trixie had seen some nice, pretty red and white flowers they could pull up.

"Come on," said Cynthia. "Let's go and unpack. We should act like we're going to stay the night."

The dragonfly soared over their heads and disappeared into an attic window.

* * *

Aunt Tabitha patted the front of her pale pink blouse.

Her stomach felt as if it were full of butterflies.

"I do hope the dinner will be a success," she said. "Everyone has worked so hard."

"So have you," said Jack.

"And I think you look simply wonderful," said Emily.

A table holding glasses of something bubbly stood in the middle of the room. Aunt Tabitha handed everyone a glass.

"I think we should drink a toast, don't you?" She raised her glass. "To Quagmire Castle Hotel!"

"Quagmire Castle Hotel!" cried everyone happily.

* * *

Cynthia Swipe squeezed her short, thick body into a frilly white dress. She looked like a wedding cake on stilts.

In front of the mirror, Eddy brushed his black hair, smeared it with gel, and wiped his hands on the back of his new shiny brown suit.

"Did you plan a signal with those kids?" Cynthia asked.

Eddy nodded. "When the bell rings for dinner to start, the kids get to work with their new toys," he said.

He grinned. "They can't wait."

"Neither can I." Cynthia got up and looked around the room.

She shook her head. "Useless dump. The sooner it's knocked down, the better."

* * *

Trixie dragged her knife across the wallpaper and pulled off a strip in her hands. "Did you call for room service?" She tore off another strip. "We can't trash the place on an empty stomach."

Norman stood on a chair and began to pull apart the lamps. "It should be here any minute," he said.

Trixie threw herself on the sofa and started poking holes in the stuffed arms. "I'm starving," she said.

"Me too," said Norman, from the bathroom. There was the sound of running water.

A minute later, he sat down beside his sister and, out of habit, pulled her hair.

She kicked him because that was what she always did. Then they ripped the cushions and hit each other on the head.

The door flew open. "Children! Children!" cried Dudley in his friendliest voice. He was wearing a long red cape and a black top hat.

"Who are you?" asked Norman. "I ordered room service, not a weirdo dressed up as a magician!"

"Indeed you did," replied Dudley.

Trixie stared at him. "If you don't have our food, get lost!"

"Yeah," said Norman, yanking a curtain off its hooks. "We got work to do."

Dudley smiled. "So have I, dear boy. So have I."

"Then hurry up," said Trixie.

She jumped up and ripped more of the wallpaper with her knife. "We're leaving this dump tonight. That's the deal."

"What deal?" asked Dudley.

"The deal we made with Mr. and Mrs. Swipe," said Norman.

Dudley threw up his hands in surprise. "There must be some mistake. What about your parents? I thought you were all on vacation."

Norman stood on the sofa and pointed at the words printed on his t-shirt. "Can't you read? **Kids Rule**! We're kids! We do what we want!"

"Yeah," said Trixie, pulling off more wallpaper. "And we never take 'no' for an answer," she said.

"Of course you don't," agreed Dudley.

He looked around the room. "But after all this hard work, aren't you getting hungry?"

"The room service is slow," said Norman. "We'll steal something from the kitchen later."

Dudley waved his red cape through the air. "Allow me to save you the trouble."

A gleaming silver food cart appeared in the middle of the room.

It was covered with hamburgers, pizzas, ice cream, and cans and cans of soft drinks.

It was exactly what Norman and Trixie ate every single day.

They rushed toward the cart, and without a word of thanks, they grabbed the food and stuffed it into their mouths like pigs.

Which was exactly what they suddenly turned into!

You could tell which one was Trixie because her pink snout was smeared with ketchup. Norman had become huge and spotted and hairy.

"Hey!" yelled his sister. "You look just like a pig!"

"You're a pig," grunted Norman.

"Don't call me a pig," screamed Trixie.

Then she saw herself in the mirror. "Norman," she said. "Look in the mirror!"

Norman turned and found himself staring at a pig wearing a **Kids Rule** t-shirt.

He gulped, then began to yell. "I want my mommy!"

"I want my daddy!" squealed Trixie. Great piggy tears rolled down her face.

"What on earth is this I see?" cried Dudley in pretend surprise. "A pair of pigs?"

A stick appeared in his hand. "We must remove them quickly before they do any more damage!"

Without another word, he herded Norman and Trixie into the hall and down the back stairs to a pigpen that suddenly appeared out of nowhere.

CHAPTER 7

Delicia stood in the dining room and stared at the amazing dinner that Dudley had made.

On one end of a long table lay a crispy roast pig with a pineapple in its mouth. At the other end was a huge fish with a knife sticking out of its head.

In between, laid out like a rainbow, were salads and dishes of every color.

In the middle, a trained octopus held up eight bowls of dip in its long arms.

"What do you think?" cried Dudley, suddenly appearing at her side.

"I like the octopus," replied Delicia.

Dudley floated around the room. "He's my favorite, too!"

Next door, there was the sound of people laughing and talking.

"Did you take care of those dreadful children?" asked Delicia.

"They're safe until it's time for them to appear," replied Dudley. "By then we'll have all the evidence Aunt Tabitha needs to put these crooks in jail."

"Jail's too good for them," cried Delicia. "I'd have them whipped and dunked in the lake."

Dudley put his finger on his wife's silver lips. "Things have changed since our day," he said.

"Ha!" said Delicia. "Cheats and liars never change."

* * *

Outside the castle, Eddy Swipe said, "There's something funny going on here."

"Don't be silly," whispered Cynthia. "Did you call Gordon?"

Eddy nodded. "He's going to meet us in the maze after we pay those kids."

"Is he bringing the papers for the old lady to sign?" Cynthia asked.

Eddy nodded, but his mind was somewhere else. He hadn't noticed the pigpen when he first looked around the castle, but he would never forget the two pigs he saw a few moments ago.

They were running back and forth in their pen, squealing at the tops of their piggy voices.

It was almost as if they were trying to tell him something.

There was something in the two little pigs' eyes that made him feel sure he had met them before.

Don't be stupid, he told himself. How can you meet a pig?

He looked up at the front of Quagmire Castle and tried to picture all the bathtubs overflowing and the water running down the walls and the ceilings falling in.

Anything to take his mind away from the look in those little pigs' eyes.

There was a tinkle of a silver spoon on a glass. On the far side of the lawn, Aunt Tabitha climbed up on a little box.

Cynthia looked around quickly. "Everyone's got a glass except us," she whispered quietly.

"And here you are," said a voice at her shoulder. Delicia held out a tray with two green glasses.

"What is it?" asked Cynthia, sniffing the glass.

"My own special treat," replied Delicia.

"About time, too," said Eddy as he grabbed a glass.

"Ladies and gentlemen," cried Aunt Tabitha. "I would like to welcome you all to Quagmire Castle Hotel! I wish you a pleasant stay and please tell all your friends about us."

She held up her glass.

"To Quagmire Castle!" she said.

"To fifty new houses!" said Eddy.

He winked at Cynthia and gulped down his drink.

He made a face. It was the strangest stuff he had ever tasted.

Cynthia swallowed her own drink and looked puzzled.

If she didn't know better, Cynthia could have sworn the liquid in her glass tasted like frog eggs. Or at least how she imagined frog eggs might taste.

"More?" asked Delicia, holding up a green bottle.

Cynthia tipped out the rest of her drink and threw her glass into the bushes. "I'll wait for dinner."

"Excellent!" replied Delicia. "You won't be disappointed!"

Across the lawn, Herbert Flubber helped Aunt Tabitha down from her box.

"Herbert! Ring the bell!" she cried. "The dinner will begin!"

Just as the bell rang, an old van roared up the driveway and screeched to a halt outside the front door.

Everyone watched as a tubby little man, dressed in a black and white sweater and wearing a mask over his face, jumped out of the van.

He pulled off the mask and quickly walked across the lawn to where Aunt Tabitha was standing.

"Good day to you, dear lady," he cried. He held out his hand. "Miss Tabitha Quagmire, I presume."

He took Aunt Tabitha's hand and kissed it. "Allow me to introduce myself. The name's Dosh. Reggie Dosh."

He flashed a smile. "What a charming place you have," he said. "May I stay here a moment, my dear?"

Even though Aunt Tabitha wasn't used to such odd events, she found herself liking this strange little man.

What's more, no one had kissed her hand for as long as she could remember.

"Of course you may!" An exciting idea popped into Aunt Tabitha's head.

"As long as you join us for dinner," said Aunt Tabitha.

"How very kind," said Reggie Dosh.

He looked over his shoulder at two raccoon faces peering out of the back window of the van.

"Would you mind if my friends came along, too?" he asked.

He waved his arm and two little men with sweet smiles pulled off their masks and jumped out.

"You see, we're making this, uh, film about honest burglars," explained Reggie Dosh.

"It's the story of this nice little guy who gets money that was stolen from him by a nasty husband and wife," he said. "After that, he starts a brand new life!"

Reggie laughed and said, "I just love happy endings!"

"How splendid!" cried Aunt Tabitha. "So do I!"

The sun sparkled on something gold and Reggie Dosh found himself looking at Eddy Swipe's front tooth.

It was a front tooth he knew well and didn't like one little bit.

A wide smile spread across Reggie Dosh's face.

Because even though he didn't believe in magic, there was something magical about this place.

Reggie was beginning to think there was a reason why his beat-up, old van had magically developed a mind of its own and sudden turned into the drive to Quagmire Castle.

Reggie Dosh took Aunt Tabitha by the arm and walked toward the front door.

Reggie was thinking that the moment had come to take care of some unfinished business with Cynthia and Eddy Swipe!

CHAPTER 8

Damian Sponge and Velveteen Gray stared at each other over the single candle that floated in a bowl of weeds and delicate wildflowers.

Usually, Velveteen Gray ordered the most expensive dish on the menu and then told the waiter at the last minute that she was a very strict vegetarian. It was her way of checking out the service at the hotels and restaurants she inspected.

But tonight was different.

Her stuffed swan and raw fish slices were delicious. They came with a dish of stewed pigs' ears. Velveteen even ate the sweet potatoes on a stick that had arrived for dessert.

Damian was amazed.

For the first time, there was color in Velveteen's cheeks, and for the first time, he noticed that she was really pretty.

"Damian," whispered Velveteen Gray. "Have I ever told you how much I like your car?"

"Gosh," cried Damian, suddenly tingling with delight. "Gosh! Do you? Do you really?"

* * *

"Gordon who?" asked Reggie Dosh.

He was convinced there was something amazing about Quagmire Castle.

He knew now why his van had roared down the drive.

He looked at Jack's serious face and put down his knife and fork.

"Gordon Grabbit," explained Jack. "He's Aunt Tabitha's bank manager."

Reggie Dosh's round face was thoughtful as he watched Aunt Tabitha laughing and talking to Sybil and Simon Breadsop on the other side of the room.

"Do you know Mr. Grabbit?" asked Emily quickly.

"I certainly do," said Reggie Dosh.

He lowered his voice. "And he wasn't a bank manager when I met him."

Jack and Emily looked at each other.

From the moment they had met this funny little man, they had both liked him a lot.

They felt they could trust him.

Jack took a deep breath, looked at Emily, and then told Reggie everything they knew about Gordon Grabbit and Cynthia and Eddy Swipe.

* * *

Cynthia Swipe played with the food on her plate and stared at her husband.

"What's wrong?" said Eddy with his mouth full. "The food's free."

He drained his glass. "Anyway, we'll be out of here any minute now."

"Something's gone wrong, Eddy," said Cynthia in a quiet voice.

She had a heavy, lumpy feeling in her stomach and she didn't like it.

"Something's wrong," she said.

"You're just looking for trouble," said Eddy, spraying pieces of roast pig all over the table.

He put down the bone he was chewing on. "Look, if it makes you feel any better, we'll leave now, pay off those brats early, and meet up with Gordon in the maze."

He turned to where Aunt Tabitha was talking to Reggie Dosh. "It won't make any difference to the old lady *when* she signs the papers, so it might as well be sooner than later."

They pushed back their chairs and were about to get up when Delicia hopped into the middle of the room and tapped a spoon against a glass.

The room fell silent.

"Ladies and gentlemen," she cried.

"We hope you enjoyed your dinner here at Quagmire Castle," said Delicia.

There was a round of applause and Damian Sponge said, "Hear, hear!"

"Marvelous!" cried Delicia.

She spun around and pointed to a pair of red curtains that hung across the far end of the room.

Everyone stared. It was amazing! No one had noticed them until that minute!

"We have a little entertainment for you," said Delicia. "I believe you will find it changes your lives forever."

A cold, sick feeling gripped Eddy for the first time.

Cynthia was right. Something was going to happen to them. And it was something bad.

"Let's get out of here now," he said.

It was too late.

The lights went down and the curtains went up. Cynthia thought she was going to be sick.

She could see Gordon Grabbit, standing in what looked like the middle of a maze.

In one hand, he held a thick brown envelope. In the other, he held a large metal flashlight.

The strange thing was that he seemed to have no idea that he was being watched by a room full of people.

"Cynthia! Eddy!" Gordon Grabbit flashed his light around the room. "Where are you?"

"Gordon," Cynthia cried. "Shut up and stop making a fool of yourself!"

Gordon didn't hear her. "Have you wrecked the place yet?" he asked.

"I've got the papers for the old lady to sign," he added quickly.

"We don't know what you're talking about," said Eddy, looking around for a way out.

"Oh, yes you do," boomed Dudley Nightshade loudly.

Two spotlights suddenly showed Trixie and Norman standing huddled together on the stage.

They weren't pigs anymore, and they weren't nasty children, either.

In fact, they looked so different, for a moment their parents did not know who they were.

"We have an announcement to make," said Norman.

"We're very ashamed of ourselves," said Trixie.

They told everyone how they planned to flood the hotel and do as much damage as they could.

Dudley stepped onto the stage. "And why did you do this?" he asked them.

Trixie and Norman lifted their arms and pointed across the room. "Because Cynthia and Eddy Swipe promised to pay us lots of money."

You could have heard a soap bubble pop. The room was silent and everyone stared as the two spotlights flashed over the tables.

The lights stopped where Cynthia and Eddy and Gordon were standing and staring at each other.

"It was Gordon's idea," shouted Cynthia. "He cheated the old lady to make her sell the castle."

Gordon Grabbit looked around him. It was as if a spell had suddenly been broken.

His sister was trying to blame everything on him again!

Well, this time, Gordon wasn't going to take it!

"It was your idea," he said to Cynthia. "And I've got the letter to prove it!"

He pulled a bright pink envelope out of his pocket. "On your special notepaper!"

"Goodness gracious," whispered Aunt Tabitha, looking around.

Reggie Dosh's bright eyes twinkled in the candlelight. "Leave it to me," he said.

Quick as a flash, Reggie jumped across the room, and snatched the two envelopes that Gordon was waving in the air.

At the same time, his two partners stood behind Gordon and Eddy and Cynthia Swipe and marched them out of the room.

"Bravo!" cried Delicia. "Let the music begin!" Out of nowhere, pretty music filled the air.

If Jack and Emily hadn't been listening extra carefully they would never have heard the police sirens outside.

"Will you dance with me?" It was Damian Sponge's voice.

Velveteen Gray smiled shyly and walked out onto the floor with Damian.

Beside them Mr. and Mrs. Breadsop were holding hands with Norman and Trixie.

And in the middle, laughing like children, Reggie Dosh spun around and around with Aunt Tabitha in his arms.

Jack and Emily sat back on their chairs and stared around at the glittering room.

Dudley and Delicia weren't there. In fact, they were nowhere to be seen.

CHAPTER 9

"Jack! Emily!"

It was the next morning and Aunt Tabitha's voice sounded excited.

Jack and Emily ran downstairs and saw their aunt holding a huge golden bell.

"It's from the hotel inspectors," she cried. "It's the highest award any hotel can win!"

Before Jack or Emily had time to speak, there was a knock on the door.

The mail carrier handed Aunt Tabitha a large white envelope.

She ripped it open, gasped, and sat down on the chair.

"Is something the matter?" cried Jack.

"I don't believe it!" cried Aunt Tabitha. She looked down at the paper.

"The bank has given me back the deeds to Quagmire Castle!" she said.

Aunt Tabitha shook her head in amazement. "Not only that, they've given me back all the money I ever paid them!"

"Good for them!" said a voice.

Reggie Dosh appeared at the door. "We can't have crooks like Gordon Grabbit and those Swipes buzzing around like greedy flies."

He grinned at Aunt Tabitha.

Then he held up a pair of goggles and a long purple scarf.

"And speaking of flying, would you come with me in my airplane? I bought it this morning," he said.

"I'd love to, Mr. Dosh," cried Aunt Tabitha. "How did you know that I loved to fly?"

She wrapped the scarf around her neck. "And purple is my favorite color."

She frowned. "But the hotel. Who will look after the hotel?" she asked.

"We'll take care of it, Aunt Tabitha," said Emily quickly.

"Are you sure?" asked her aunt.

"Of course," said Jack.

Aunt Tabitha still looked worried. "What about those two lovely people?"

She shook her head. "I never thanked them and they just disappeared."

Emily laughed.

"They'll be around if we need them, Aunt Tabitha," said Emily.

Jack and Emily watched as Reggie Dosh helped Aunt Tabitha into a shiny red plane that bobbed gently on Toad Lake.

They had never seen their aunt look so happy.

"Bye!" she cried. She blew them a kiss and the plane's engines started up with a giant roar.

* * *

Jack and Emily walked up the front steps of Quagmire Castle. They stood in the hall.

All the guests had gone.

"Whew!" said Jack, falling back in a chair and letting his legs swing over the side.

"What an adventure!" he said.

He turned to Emily, who was staring at the wall at the far end of the hallway.

"Do you know what?" said Jack. "I figured out that Delicia and Dudley are probably our great-great-great-great-great-grandparents."

Emily burst out laughing. "Jack!" she cried. "Look at the paintings!"

Jack turned and started to laugh, too.

On the wall, Delicia and Dudley stared at them out of their paintings. They were grinning.

And Powderball crossed his eyes and stuck out his tongue at them!

ABOUT THE AUTHOR

Karen Wallace is the author of more than one hundred books for children, and the winner of several book awards. She was born in Canada and grew up in a log cabin in the woods of Quebec. She has also lived in France and Ireland, and has worked making pizzas, and singing in a cabaret and a bluegrass band. Writing is her favorite activity. Wallace says she has spent most of her life making up stories.

GLOSSARY

deed (DEED)—a legal paper that tells who owns a piece of property

maze (MAYZ)—a confusing and winding set of pathways. Some people grow a garden maze, with paths that wander between high bushes or hedges.

quagmire (KWAYG-mire)— a swamp, or a difficult situation

spell (SPELL)—a group of words that some believe have magical power

suspicious (sus-PISH-uhss)—uncertain or not trusting someone

vulture (VUHL-chur)—a kind of large bird with dark feathers and a bare neck. Vultures feed on dead animals.

DISCUSSION QUESTIONS

1. Emily is always noticing people's eyes or "something in their eyes." What is meant by that? What can you tell about a person by looking in their eyes?

2. Why was Reggie Dosh wearing a mask when he appeared at Quagmire Castle? And why do you think he took it off when he met Aunt Tabitha?

3. Cynthia Swipe says the only way to make money is "the dirty way." What does she mean by that? And how do you feel about people who make money that way?

WRITING PROMPTS

1. If you had magical powers like Dudley and Delicia, how would you used them to help save Aunt Tabitha's castle?

2. Dudley liked turning into animals. What would be your favorite animal to change into? Write and tell us how it feels to be that animal. Describe how you move and eat, and tell us what you can see and hear.

3. Jack and Emily discover the secret home of the ghosts after they follow Powderball up a strange set of steps they have never seen before. What if you found a new door or stairway in your home? Write and tell us where it would lead you.

ALSO BY
KAREN WALLACE

Something Slimy on Primrose Drive

Boris and Anaconda Wolfbane move from their swamp home to a house on Primrose Drive. They dream of a safe, ordinary life for their family. But the Wolfbanes are far from ordinary.

Aargh, It's an Alien!

Albert's parents give him everything he wants, except time with them. Can the aliens find a way to make Albert's life more fun?

OTHER PATHWAY BOOKS

Time and Again
by Rob Childs

Becky and Chris discover a strange-looking watch with the power to travel back through time. Time travel is not as easy as they thought, especially when class troublemaker Luke decides to join them.

James and the Alien Experiment
S. Prue

When James is abducted by aliens, he undergoes some drastic changes. His new super strength, super brains, and super speed, however, bring more problems than James bargained for.